Hello Doggy!

HarperCollins *Children's Books*

Round the corner, not far away, Bing and Flop are going to the park today.

Bing and Flop play with the ball.

Hup!

Hup!

Oops!

Bing throws the ball **really** far.

"Hello, Doggy!"

Bing wants to play with the dog.

Flop shows Bing how to make friends with the dog.

"We need to be nice and quiet. Then you hold your hand out low so the dog can smell you."

"There we are. Now, you come and make friends too, Bing."

Hello, doggy!

"He's wagging his tail!"

"I think he likes you, Bing."

"Good doggy," says Bing, gently stroking the dog. "What's your name?"

Flop looks at the dog's collar. "Hmm...there's no name tag."

Woof!

"Can we keep him?" asks Bing.

"Sorry, Bing. We can't keep him, but we **can** look after him until his owner comes back."

The ball lands behind a bush.

"What's the doggy doing?" asks Bing.

"I think he's going to smell
where the ball went," says Flop.

Flop puts the poo
in a special poo bin.

"When you have a dog,
you have to do the
yucky stuff as well
as the fun stuff, Bing."

"But **not** in
the **park!**"

"We'll need to wash
our hands when we
get home."

The dog gives Bing a playful lick.
"Aww...he **loves** me, Flop!"

"Yes, he does."

"Can we keep him NOW, Flop?"

"Sorry, Bing, we still can't keep him. He's not ours."

"Oh, but he's my friend," says Bing sadly.

Bing! Flop!

"Look!" says Flop. "It's Gilly and Popsie."

"Hello, Bing. Oh, you've found Sunshine.
Thank you for looking after her."

"Oh! Sunshine is a girl dog," says Bing.

Woof!

Woof!

"Yes, she's Popsie's sister," says Gilly.

"And she's my friend," says Bing.

"Yes, I can see she really likes you, Bing.
Would you like to play with her next week?"

"Ooh! Yes, please!"

"Time to go home now, Sunshine.
Bing, would you like to hold her lead?"

Hi!

I saw a **doggy** in the park. She's called **Sunshine**.

You have to let a doggy **smell you** to make friends, and then you can play catch together.

Woof!

I wanted to keep the doggy. But Flop said we couldn't because she's not ours, and then I was **sad**.

Oh!

But then Gilly came and said I can play with her **next week** because she's my **new friend**.

Dogs...

they're a Bing thing.